THE BOX BOYS

AND THE DOG IN THE MIST

Jenny Nimmo

Illustrated by Anthony Lewis

a division of Hodder Headline plc

Published in Great Britain in 1999 by
Hodder Children's Books

10 9 8 7 6 5 4 3 2 1

A Catalogue record for this book is available from the British Library

ISBN 0 340 73293 8

Printed and bound in Great Britain by
Guernsey Press, Channel Islands

Hodder Children's Books
a division of Hodder Headline plc
338 Euston Road
London NW1 3BH

For the children and staff of
Rhayader Church in Wales School

Chapter One

It was five days after Christmas. Scott Box and his friend, John, were sitting in Scott's bedroom, staring out of the window at the sky. It was dark and grey. The boys didn't want to play outside, it was so muddy. They seemed to have run out of things to do.

"I wish something exciting would happen," said Scott.

"Perhaps we should close our eyes and make a wish," said John.

There was something special about John and Scott. They'd been born on the same day, in the same year, and they had the same surname - Box.

And they lived next door to each other. Sometimes when they were together, strange things happened to John and Scott.

The boys were about to close their eyes and wish, when Scott's mum came into his room.

"Guess what!" she said. "We're all going on holiday!"

"Holiday?" said Scott. "I hope we're going somewhere warm - the weather's horrible!"

"Well . . . no . . ." said Mrs Box, "we're going somewhere even colder than this. We're going to the Welsh mountains."

"Brilliant!" said the Box boys.

"When are we going?" asked Scott.

"Tomorrow. We'll spend New Year's Eve in a little cottage in the mountains."

"What is New Year's Eve exactly?" asked John.

"The night this year turns into next year," said Scott's mum. "It happens on the stroke of midnight."

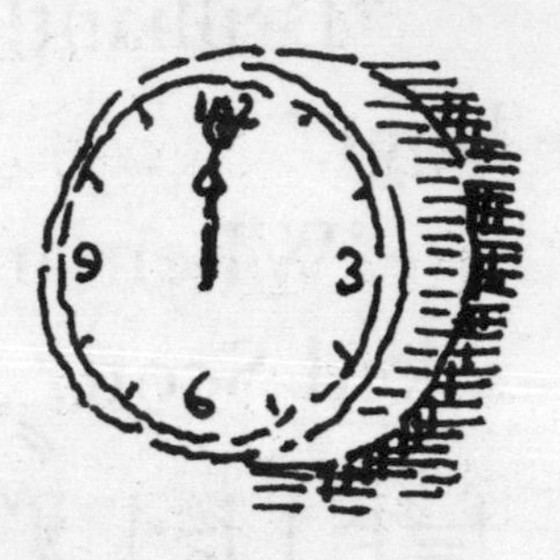

"I'm going to get packed," said John. He rushed past Scott's mum and down the stairs.

"Our wish came true!" Scott called after him.

"And we didn't even make a wish," John reminded him.

When he got home, John's mum was making a list of the things they needed to take on holiday. "It's just a short trip," she told John. "Just a weekend in the snow."

"Snow?!" said John.

"Well, there might be snow on the mountains," she said. "There usually is at this time of year. We'll go in two cars so there'll be plenty of room for extras, like blankets and food."

"What about Bunk? Can he come?" asked John.

His mum shook her head. "No dog's allowed, I'm afraid. It's sheep country. The ewes will be having their lambs next month and we don't want Bunk to start chasing them."

"He wouldn't," said John. "And he'd love running over the fields."

"He's not a sheepdog, John," said his mum. "We'll have to leave him with Gran. He loves it there."

John thought he'd better not tell his dog what was happening, though sometimes Bunk seemed to know if John was going away. Today, he was lying by the fire in the sitting room.

His head was on his paws and he looked very sleepy. He looked up and whined when John came in.

John stroked Bunk's head. "I wish you'd got a friend to go out with, like I've got Scott," he said. "Wouldn't it be great if Scott had a dog, too."

Bunk gave a little grunt. John was sure he understood.

Next morning Scott called round early for John. They took Bunk to John's granny, who lived at the end of the road. She was waiting for Bunk with a bag of his special chocolate treats.

Bunk gave a little bark of excitement and ran into her house.

"Have a good time," she said to the boys, "and don't get lost in those Welsh mists."

The two cars were packed and ready when the Box Boys got home. They were travelling together in John's car first. Then they would meet up with Scott's parents for a motorway snack and travel the rest of the way with them.

Most of the journey was boring and the Box Boys fell asleep after the halfway snack.

They woke up to hear Scott's dad say, "Look, boys!"

The Box Boys looked out to see the mountains, huge and dark, rising on all sides.

The sun was a fiery globe sinking behind a range of jagged mountains, like a dragon's back.

Even as the boys watched, the sun slipped below the mountains, and in its rosy light they could see that the highest peaks were covered in snow.

"Can we go up there, Dad?" asked Scott. "Up to the top?"

"We'll see what the weather's like," said his father. "We don't want to get caught in a snowstorm."

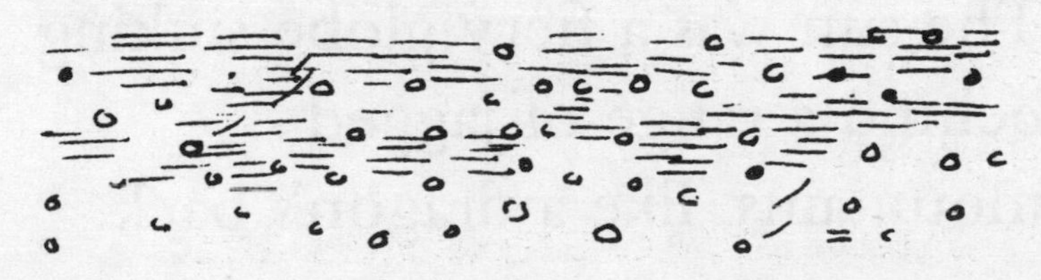

Chapter Two

The cottage was small, but very cosy. Scott and John had to share a room, which they wanted to anyway.

After they'd unpacked and

had their supper, the Box Boys ran up to their room. They were so excited that they couldn't sleep. They whispered together and then listened to the strange silence. It wa so different from home.

They heard an owl hoot, and a rustling stream. They even heard a vixen cry out and then, in the distance, a strange sort of howling.

"Did you hear that?" whispered John.

"Yes. What was it?"

"I don't know, but it

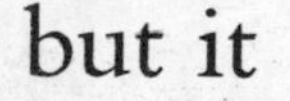

sounded a bit ghostly."

Scott shivered and dived under his blankets. John did the same.

They must have fallen asleep after that because the next thing they knew, a bright shaft of sunlight was sliding through the curtains.

The Box Boys jumped out of bed and pulled on their clothes. Downstairs they found their mums frying bacon and sausages.

"We forgot the bread," laughed John's mum.

"So did we," said Scott's mum, "and the butter."

"We'll go into town," said Scott's dad. "We need some more food for our New Year's party."

It was decided that John's mum and dad would go walking with the boys, while Scott's parents did the shopping.

After breakfast, both families called in on their neighbour, old Mrs Ellis, who looked after the cottage when it was empty.

Mrs Ellis was a merry, twinkly old woman, but when she heard the boys were going walking, and perhaps climbing, she took one look at their feet and said, "You can't go walking in wellies, my dears. You need some proper walking boots. You wait there and I'll go and find some." She bustled off and came back with several pairs of sturdy boots.

"People are always leaving them behind," she said. "Then the children's feet grow and they don't want their boots back. See if these'll fit."

The Box Boys tried on several pairs and at last they each found a pair that fitted. The bounced up and down, proud of their new footwear.

"Brilliant! Thank you!" they cried.

"You'd better be off soon then," said Mrs Ellis. "If you want to get back safely. There's a mist coming down so I've heard. It's sunny now, but it can change very suddenly in the mountains, you know."

"We'll take care," said John's dad. "We've got a map, so we won't get lost, but thanks for the warning."

"If you do get lost you might see the ghost dog," said Mrs Ellis.

"The ghost dog?" The Box Boys wanted to know more, but Mrs Ellis just waved her hand, smiling, and closed the door.

The Boxes set off; four up the mountains; two into town.

The weather was perfect. Windy and cold, but very sunny. John wished Bunk could have come.

But when they saw a field of fat, nervous sheep, he understood why Bunk had needed to stay behind - he would probably have chased them.

They crossed a stream by way of a small stone bridge, and then they began to climb. The path was narrow and steep. Mr Box went first, John came next, then

Scott and last of all, John's mum.

"I'm afraid we can't have sandwiches," she said. "But I've got loads of cake and bananas and apples in my backpack. We'll stop for a break in about an hour."

The Box Boys were hungry already. Up they went. Up and up and up. Across a sloping field, then up again until they reached a wide, rocky place –

perfect for a picnic.

They sat on a rock and watched the sheep move slowly on the sloping fields.

They saw a rabbit and a huge bird hovering in the sky. "A buzzard," said John's dad.

Far, far away they could see their cottage. It looked smaller than a matchbox.

"Shall we go on, or have you had enough?" asked Mr Box.

"On!" cried the Box Boys. "Let's go on!"

They shook their crumbs on to the rocks "for the birds," said John's mum, and then they carried on walking. This time, they crossed a wide stretch of bracken. John's mum couldn't keep up with them and when John looked round to call her she was just a speck in a great white cloud. A mist had crept up, and everything behind them had vanished.

"I think we'd better go back," said John's dad. "I hope we can find the path again."

Chapter Three

John and Scott raced through the bracken until they reached John's mum.

"This is horrible," she said. "I can hardly see a thing."

"I think the path begins over there," said Mr Box, pointing behind her.

They walked first one way, then another, trying to find their way back to the picnic rock, but the path had disappeared. When they looked up at the sky, all they could see was a dark, dark cloud. No sun, no blue sky.

"The mist came down so suddenly," said John's mum.

"Mrs Ellis said it could," John reminded her.

Then they heard a bark.

"A sheepdog!" cried John. "Perhaps there's a farmer with him. He'll know the way."

They stood still for a minute,

listening. And then it came again; a high-pitched sort of howl.

"It's like the sound we heard last night," said Scott. "It's sort of . . . ghostly."

They walked towards where the bark seemed to be coming from, but now the mist was so thick that they could hardly see the ground in front of them.

"Sshh," said John. "I thought I saw something move. This way."

"Be careful, John," called his mother. "You can't see where you're going."

But it was too late.

John had leapt too far and, "Ouch!" he slid into a stream.

He couldn't keep his balance and rolled into the water. "Oooh!" he moaned. "It's freezing!"

Scott ran over and pulled him out.

"Oooh," groaned John again. "I think that dog is trying to trick us."

"Is it?" said Scott. "Maybe it's just trying to help us?"

Then they heard the bark again.

"It's over there," said Scott, pointing ahead.

This time they walked more slowly, testing the ground ahead as they went, and they found the beginning of the path. It had been easy climbing up, but going down in a thick mist was almost impossible. They slid and stumbled on loose stones, clutching the bank and tufts of wild grass. After some time, Mrs Box said, "Where's our picnic place? We should have reached it by now. This is all wrong."

Then there was another bark.

"It's not wrong," said John's dad. "Just follow the bark."

Sure enough, they soon came to to the rock where they'd eaten their picnic.

But now which way should they go? The next path had completely disappeared.

Another bark. This time from right below them.

"Down here," said John. "I've found the way."

On they went, slowly, carefully, feeling their way; sometimes falling and sliding on their bottoms. But all the time, there was the strange ghostly bark to lead them on.

It took a long long time and John's clothes were wet and heavy. His teeth were chattering and he began to sneeze.

"We'll be home soon, John," said Scott. But he wasn't completely sure about that.

Then, suddenly, just as he was starting to think he'd never be warm again, Scott slipped off the path.

He found himself rolling down and down and down.

He landed with a bump. For a moment he felt dizzy and then he realised that the mist was beginning to clear and there, right in front of him, stood a dog; a black sheepdog with two white paws.

Chapter Four

"Hello," said Scott. "Are you . . . are you the ghost dog?"

The sheepdog gave a low whine and wagged his tail. But then he started to disappear into the background, until he was just a misty little cloud, drifting away.

"Scott! Scott! Where are you!?" called John's mum.

"Here!" Scott called back. "I'm in a field. The mist has gone and I can see for miles." He stood up. "In fact, I can see our cottage."

"Hurray!" In a second John had rolled down beside him.

It took his mum and dad a bit longer. They didn't feel like rolling, so they came down on the path.

“I saw the dog,” said Scott.

“Did you?” cried John. “I wish I had.”

“It was a black sheepdog, with two white feet.”

“I wonder where he went,” said John’s mum. “Come on, let’s get you two home.”

After tea, when they were dry and warm again, Scott asked if he could go and see Mrs Ellis.

"I want to tell her about the dog," he said.

"I'll come with you," said John.

Mrs Ellis took a long time to answer. The boys were about to give up knocking when she suddenly opened the door. "Sorry, boys," she said. "I don't hear too well these days."

"We wanted to know about the ghost dog," Scott said. "Is it black with two white feet."

"That's him," said Mrs Ellis. "They called him Non. He saved

his master's life, so
the story goes.
His master was
a very old
farmer and he
was out in the
snow with his
ewes when he fell
and broke his leg. Non rall
all the way to the
village to fetch
help. He
wouldn't stop
barking until
they'd found
the old man and
carried him back
home."

"When did it happen?" asked John.

"About a hundred years ago," said Mrs Ellis.

"Wow," said the Box Boys. "So he really *is* a ghost."

"Oh, yes," she yawned sleepily. "Now, I think I'm ready for bed . . . goodnight boys."

The Box Boys said goodnight and went back to tell their parents the story of Non the sheepdog. They were so tired that they fell asleep well before midnight. And if their parents did have a New Year's Eve party, John and Scott didn't hear a thing. Not even a ghostly howl would have woken them that night.

The next day was the first day of the New Year. Scott made a promise: to have a dog. John couldn't decide what his New Year's promise should be.

Both families set off early for another day's walking - this time they made piles of sandwiches to take with them. They walked and walked, and climbed and climbed.

They saw buzzards and rabbits, sheep and squirrels, even a fox.

But they never saw Non the sheepdog. It was still a brilliant day, though.

Exhausted they arrived back to spend one more night in the cottage They were driving home the next day.

Before they left, the boys went to say goodbye to old Mrs Ellis.

"Have a good journey," she said. "And come again."

"We definitely will," said Scott. "And I hope I see Non again."

"I hope you don't," said Mrs Ellis. "He only appears when folk are in trouble."

"I really do want a dog," Scott told John as the car sped south and lights and cities began to appear.

"Bunk would like it, too," said John. "He needs a friend."

When they got home John and Scott rushed round to John's granny's to fetch Bunk.

As soon as Granny Box opened the door Bunk flew into John's arms.

"He's missed you dreadfully," she said. "To tell the truth he gave me a bit of a fright. Come in and I'll tell you about it."

The boys and Bunk sat in Granny Box's kitchen, eating cake, while she told them about how Bunk had run away.

"He rushed out of the house when I opened the door to the postman," she said. "I searched

everywhere and asked all
the neighbours to
look out for
him. At
teatime the
doorbell
rang. I
opened the
door and
there was
Bunk - with a
tall red-haired boy. 
He said his name was Pete and
he'd found Bunk digging a hole
in his garden. Pete's mum told
him I was looking for a dog."

"Pete?" said John. "We
know him. He's really mean."

"Perhaps he's changed," said Granny Box.

The boys thanked her for the cake and led Bunk home to John's house.

Scott was just about to run into his own house when he remembered something.

"It's our birthdays on Wednesday," he said.

"Oh yeah. We've been so busy I'd forgotten. What do you want?"

"Guess?"

John knew what Scott wanted. "I want roller blades," he said.

On Wednesday morning, John ran next door with a present for Scott. Scott's mum let him in. There was a large box in the hall with a card on it. "*For Scott*", it said.

Inside something was moving and scratching.

"Scott, come downstairs," called his mum. "John's here . . . and a mysterious box has arrived for you."

Scott appeared at the top of the stairs. He dashed down in five seconds flat.

"Happy Birthday!" the Box Boys chorused to each other.

Scott knelt by the box amd opened the top.

He gasped, "I don't believe it!" and lifted out a puppy. It was black with two white paws.

"I'm going to call him Non," said Scott, hugging the puppy. "After the ghost dog that helped us in the mist!"